W9-CGP-502

Sunflower Sal

Janet S. Anderson
Illustrated by Elizabeth Johns

Albert Whitman & Company ✳ Morton Grove, Illinois

Also by Janet S. Anderson:
The Key into Winter

✳

Anderson, Janet, 1946-
Sunflower Sal / written by Janet S. Anderson;
illustrated by Elizabeth Johns.
p. cm.
Summary: Sal, a very big girl, cannot sew a quilt like Gran's no matter
how hard she tries, but eventually she finds that her talents lie elsewhere.
ISBN 0-8075-7662-X
[1. Sunflowers–Fiction. 2. Size–Fiction. 3. Country life–Fiction.]
I. Johns, Elizabeth, 1943- ill. II. Title.
PZ7.A5365Su 1997
[E]–dc21   96-53906
                                                CIP
                                                AC

Text copyright ©1997 by Janet S. Anderson.
Illustrations copyright © 1997 by Elizabeth Johns.
Published in 1997 by Albert Whitman & Company,
6340 Oakton Street, Morton Grove, Illinois 60053-2723.
Published simultaneously in Canada by
General Publishing, Limited, Toronto.
All rights reserved. No part of this book may be
reproduced or transmitted in any form or by any means,
electronic or mechanical, including photocopying, recording,
or by any information storage and retrieval system, without
permission in writing from the publisher.
Printed in the United States of America.
10   9   8   7   6   5   4   3

The illustrations were painted in oil on canvas.
The text typeface is Clearface
and the display face is New York.
Designed by Karen A. Yops.

To John, Kate, and Alix, who always think big,
and to Kay, who planted the seed.   J.S.A.

For my mother and my daughter, who taught me the joy of putting
a seed in the earth and waiting for the miracle.   E.J.

SAL was a big girl. She was bigger than Gran. She was bigger than Ma. She wasn't as big as Pa yet, but she was getting there.

"How's my big girl?" Pa would ask proudly when
she'd bring the cider jug out to the field in the afternoons.
"Good, Pa," Sal would reply, because mostly she was.

Mostly she liked being big. She could reach the best apples in the orchard and shake the most nuts out of the hickory tree. She could jump ditches and rescue kittens and swim to the blackberry patch across the river in no time flat.

And all her friends agreed that nobody could build a
snowman quite like Sal.

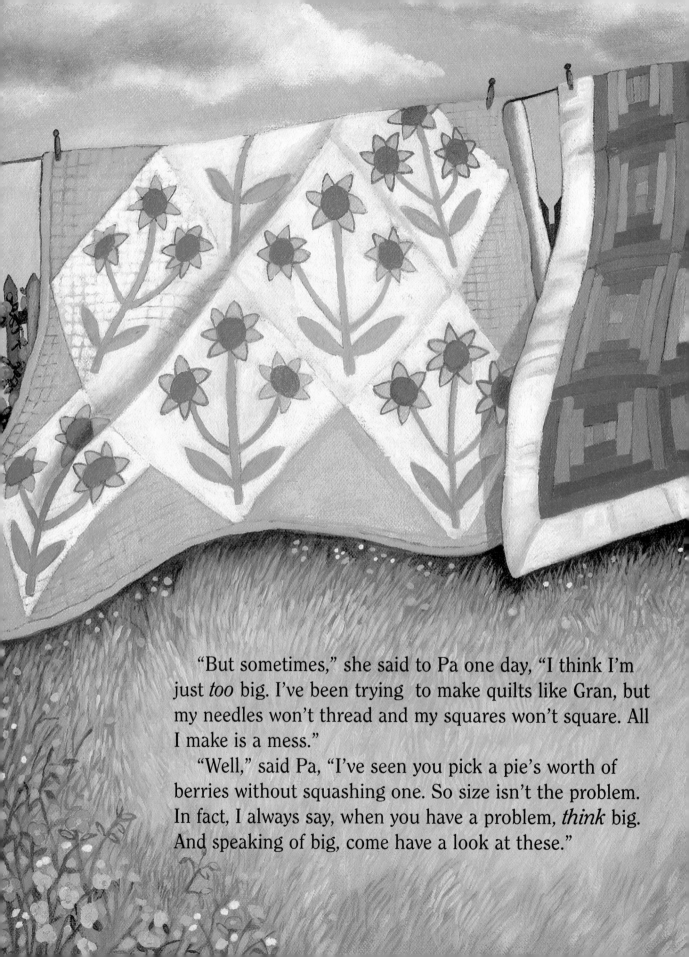

"But sometimes," she said to Pa one day, "I think I'm just *too* big. I've been trying to make quilts like Gran, but my needles won't thread and my squares won't square. All I make is a mess."

"Well," said Pa, "I've seen you pick a pie's worth of berries without squashing one. So size isn't the problem. In fact, I always say, when you have a problem, *think* big. And speaking of big, come have a look at these."

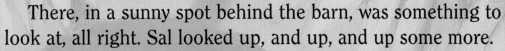

There, in a sunny spot behind the barn, was something to look at, all right. Sal looked up, and up, and up some more.

"Giant sunflowers," said Pa. "Look at those seedheads. Why, we'll be eating on those seeds all next winter."

But Sal wasn't looking at seedheads. She was looking at color, the swirl of gold and tawny brown and coppery green that towered above and around her. It was so beautiful she almost couldn't breathe.

"Pa," she said when she could finally speak, "could I have some of those seeds? Could I *plant* them?"

"Why, sure," said Pa. "Plant as many as you want."

Sal did. The next spring she planted a big patch beside the back door. "Sal," Ma said as the summer slipped by, "they're real pretty, but I can't get *out*. Try someplace else."

Sal did. The next spring she planted a bigger patch out behind the garden. "Sal," said Gran as the summer wore on, "they're the prettiest things I ever saw, but they're shading my beans. Try someplace else."

Sal did. The next spring she planted two long rows, one on each side of the lane. The sunflowers grew tall and gold, tawny brown and coppery green, and even if you turned off the road in a bad mood, you were smiling by the time you got to the house.

"Now *that's* thinking big," said Pa.

"But it's not a quilt," said Sal. The next winter she tried one more time. But her needles still wouldn't thread, and her squares still wouldn't square. "I'm just too big," she said to Gran sadly. "Too big and clumsy."

Gran shook her head. "Can't be that," she said. "I've seen you plant a row of seeds without dropping one. No, Sal, it's just that your talent isn't sewing. It's sunflowers. Stick to sunflowers."

So Sal did. The next spring she planted the lane and kept on going. Every day after school, she walked up and down the dusty roads, her sunbonnet full of seeds, her trowel at the ready. She loved the feel of dirt between her fingers and warm sun on her back. She loved planting sunflowers.

All summer she watched them grow. And as they grew, the corn slowly ripened. The tomatoes fattened on their vines, and the hayfields readied for one last cutting.

"Picnic time," said Ma. "We all need a rest before the harvest comes in."

"Where should we go, Sal?" asked Pa. "Think big, now."

"Bare Hill," said Sal. "That's the biggest thing around."

They hitched up the team and filled the wagon with baskets of food, jugs of cider, and Gran's old quilts for sitting.

They drove up and around and up
and around to the top of Bare Hill.
They spread the quilts and ate
their fill. Then they all lay down and
had a good rest in the warmth and
buzz of the sunny meadow.

Just before leaving, they walked up the steep trail to the peak. They looked down. The land below them, shining in the late afternoon sun, was the familiar pattern of cornfields, hayfields, pasture, and farm lot they'd gazed at for years.

But this year it was different.

Pa looked puzzled. Ma looked puzzled. But Sal and Gran just looked. Then, laughing, they whirled each other up into a joyful hug.

"Oh, Gran," said Sal. She stood as tall as she could and
stretched out her arms. "I did it, didn't I?"
"You sure did," said Gran. "Big as life and twice as pretty."

The patches of farmland were outlined now by threads
of gold and tawny brown and coppery green. The land
itself had been stitched together with sunflowers.

"A quilt," said Sal. "I finally made a quilt."